for David, Aubrey, and Avery

Published by Octobre Press
736-22nd Place, Vero Beach, FL 32960

www.PansyAtThePalace.com

Illustrations created by Kim Weissenborn
Editorial Development provided by Lisa Pliscou
Art Direction and Publishing Management provided by Libby Ellis

Special thanks to Ginger and Monny.

PRINTED IN THE UNITED STATES

This book was typeset in Berkeley.
These charming illustrations were created using pen & ink, and watercolor!

ISBN: 978-0-615-69253-1

Manufactured by Thomson-Shore, Dexter, MI (USA); RMA584TB980, October, 2012

Pansy at the Palace

A Beverly Hills Mystery

written by Cynthia Bardes

illustrations by Kim Weissenborn

Once upon a time, I lived at an animal shelter in Los Angeles. Every day I watched other dogs go home with new families.

Some people wanted a big dog. Some people wanted a medium dog.
And some wanted a little dog. But no one wanted me.

Then one day, I saw a little girl who had brown curly hair just like mine. She looked at me and smiled. I jumped up and barked. I pressed my nose against the bars. The little girl walked over to my cage. "Her face looks just like a pansy!" she said. "Please, may I hold her?" I snuggled up to her. I gave her as many kisses as I could. I loved her the minute she held me.

"Can we take her home with us, Mama?" the little girl asked. The lady smiled and answered, "Of course. We'll adopt her." "I'm going to call her Pansy," the little girl said.

I couldn't believe it! Someone wanted me at last! My new life was beginning!

We arrived at the Palace Hotel in Beverly Hills. A man
in a beautiful jacket with gold buttons opened the car door.
"Hello, Roberto," Avery said. "This is Pansy." "Good afternoon,
Pansy," Roberto said. "Welcome to the Palace." Was I dreaming?
Would this be my new home?

We went inside. Avery showed me the Tea Room. People were drinking tea and eating fancy cakes.

Next to the Tea Room was the Bijoux Boutique. It was full of sparkling jewelry. "Hello, Mr. Bijoux. This is Pansy," Avery said. "Bonjour, Pansy," said Mr. Bijoux. "You will be a lovely addition to our hotel family."

Avery took me to our suite. "This is where I sleep," Avery said. "You will have your bed right next to mine. Oh, Pansy, it's so much fun living in a hotel! I have a book about a little girl in New York who lives in a hotel, too. I'll read it to you."

In the morning, Avery and I ate breakfast on the hotel roof by the pool.

We played all morning. I loved my new life.

Every day, Avery and I went for our walk. We saw people and shops, trees and flowers. There was so much to see.

One day, when we came back to the hotel, I saw a big white cat.
I sniffed. The cat had a fishy smell. She arched her back and hissed
at me. I crept close to Avery. "Don't worry, Pansy," Avery told me.
"That is Desirée. She belongs to Monsieur DuMal." Monsieur DuMal
said, "Do not hiss, my dear. That is a charming little poodle."
I sniffed again. There was something peculiar about Desirée.

The next day, when Avery was out with her mother, I saw Desirée slinking along the hall. I smelled that fishy smell again. I was curious. I decided to follow her. I watched Desirée sneak through the kitchen doors.

"Hello, Pansy," the chef said. "How nice of you to visit. Desirée likes to visit us, too. She loves salmon." Desirée looked at me and hissed.

That night, while I was sleeping, I heard a loud noise outside. Avery and I woke up. We ran to the French doors. We saw Desirée hanging from a branch. She glared. How peculiar!

The next morning, a lady flung open the door to her room and shrieked, "My jewels! They're gone!" Another lady opened her door and screamed, "My jewels are gone, too!" "This is simply shocking!" exclaimed Mr. Garrett, the manager. He called the Beverly Hills police.

When the police arrived, they searched high and low. Nervous guests waited in the lobby. The hotel had a thief! "Who could it be, Mr. Garrett?" Avery asked. "I don't know," Mr. Garrett replied. "If we can't find the missing jewelry and

the thief, the guests will leave! The hotel will be ruined!" "Oh, Pansy, what will we do?" Avery said. "Our beautiful hotel might close. Everyone will lose their jobs." She looked very sad. That made me sad, too.

Mr. Bijoux came rushing out of his shop. "My most valuable diamond necklace was stolen!" he cried.

A policeman looked around the shop. I sniffed the air. There was that fishy smell again. "If only we had a clue!" the policeman said. Suddenly there was a purring sound. Desirée jumped off the bench and scampered away.

Something was strange about that cat. I took off after her!

I followed the fishy smell. I came to a door. I pushed it open with my nose.

Desirée hissed at me from the bed. I turned to leave, but suddenly I saw something. Something shiny. Something glittery. I knew what it was!

I ran to the bed and tugged at it with my teeth. *Yes!* It was Mr. Bijoux's diamond necklace! I grabbed the necklace and dashed out the door.

I ran to Avery. "Look!" Avery cried. "Pansy found the necklace!"
The policeman asked, "Where did you find it, Pansy?"

I barked and ran back to the room. "It's Monsieur DuMal's room!" shouted
Mr. Bijoux. "They're trying to escape!" the policeman yelled. *"Stop!"*

"Monsieur DuMal," cried Avery. "Did you take Mr. Bijoux's diamond necklace?" Monsieur DuMal hung his head. He confessed that he had trained Desirée to sneak into the rooms and steal jewels, and then rewarded her with salmon.

That evening, everyone gathered in the lobby to celebrate. "Pansy, you are a hero!" said Mr. Garrett. "You saved the Palace Hotel!" "She's the very best dog in the world!" exclaimed Mr. Bijoux. Avery hugged me. "Pansy," she said, "I love you."